OLIVIA
forms a band

To Tonia, who saved my life

SIMON AND SCHUSTER
First published in Great Britain in 2006
by Simon and Schuster UK Ltd
1st Floor, 222 Gray's Inn Road,
London WC1X 8HB
A CBS Company
This paperback edition published in 2009
Originally published in 2006 by Atheneum
books for Young Readers, an imprint of
Simon & Schuster Children's Publishing
Division, New York

Book design by Ann Bobco
The text for this book is set in Centaur.
The illustrations for this book are rendered in
charcoal and gouache on paper.
A CIP catalogue record for this book is
available from the British Library upon request

Printed in Italy
10 9 8 7 6 5 4 3 2 1
ISBN 978 1 84738 604 5

OLIVIA
forms a band

by Ian Falconer

SIMON AND SCHUSTER
London   New York   Sydney

Olivia couldn't find her other red sock.

"What's the matter?" asked her mother.
"I can't find my other red sock," said Olivia.
"What are those all over the floor?"
"They don't go with this one."

"I found it!"

Olivia's mother was packing a picnic.
"I want everyone ready by seven
for the fireworks," she said.
"And the band!" cried Olivia.

"Oh, I don't think there will
be a band," said her mother.

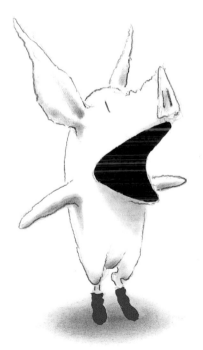

"But you can't have fireworks
without a band," explained Olivia.

"Fine," said Olivia. "I'll be the band."

"What kind of band
are you thinking of?"
asked her mother.

"A fireworks band,
of course."

"But, sweetheart, one person can't be a
whole band," said Olivia's mother.
"Why not?"
"Because the word 'band' means more than
one person, and a band *sounds* like more
than one person."

"This morning you told me
I sounded like five people!"

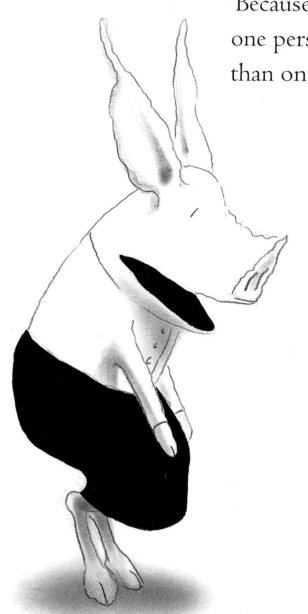

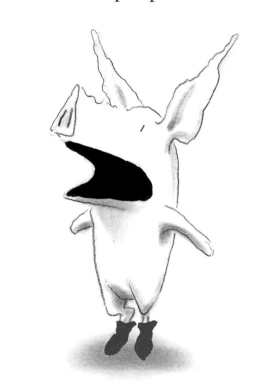

All day long Olivia gathered everything she needed to make her band.

"Thank you."

"Thank you."

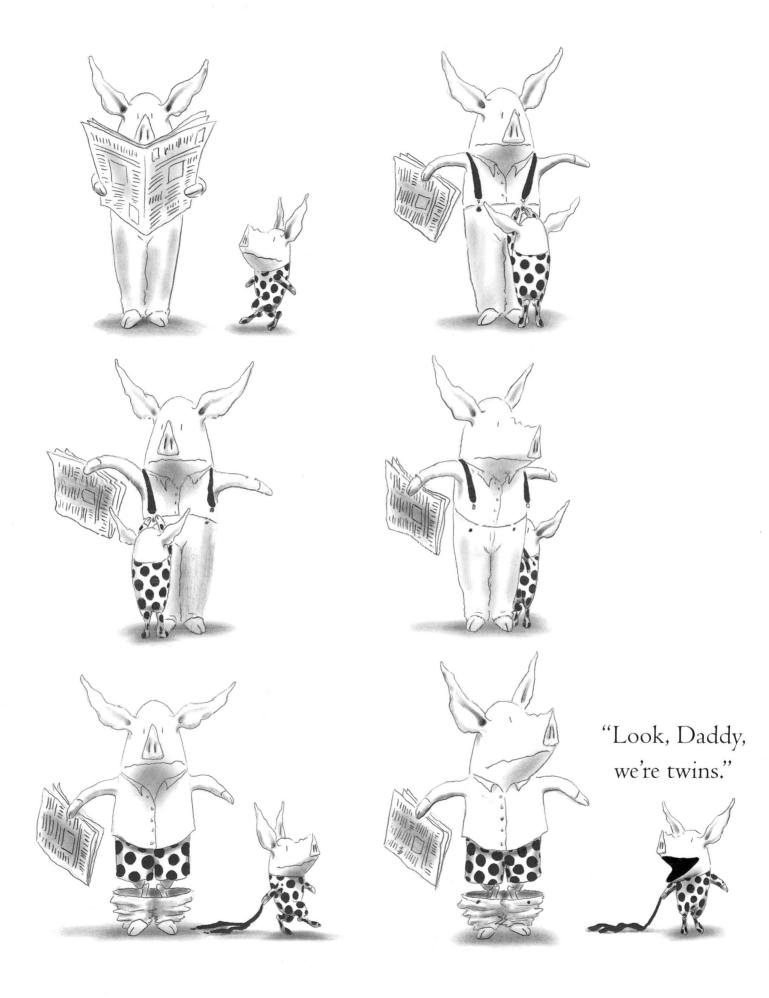

"Look, Daddy,
we're twins."

Finally she was finished.
All that was left was to choose the perfect outfit.

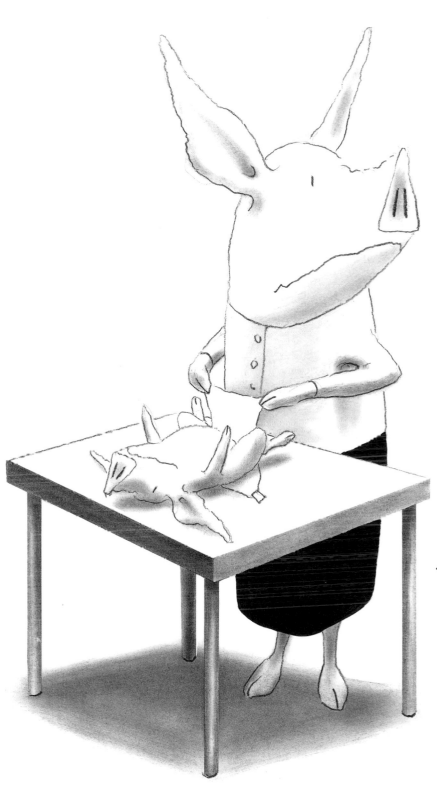

And when she marched in, everyone agreed that
Olivia *did* sound like more than one person.

TING
WHIIIISTLE
CLANG
DONG
PANK PINK PONK
BOOM
TING
WHISSSTLE
TING
CLANG
TOINK
TING
DING
BOOM
DING
DONGGG

To Olivia, she sounded just like a real band.

At seven o'clock Olivia's mother was trying to get everyone into the car. "Olivia, aren't you going to bring your band?" she asked.

"I don't feel like it."

"Well, don't forget to put everything away,"
 her mother said.
"Okay, Mummy."
"Where are you going?"
"I have to put on my make-up," said Olivia.
"All right, sweetheart, but hurry."

The final touch . . .

"Wipe that glop off your face, young lady, and get in the car NOW!"

Of course, when they got there . . .

Olivia said,
"Mummy,
I have to go
to the
bathroom."

And, of course,
then Ian said
he had
to go to the
bathroom too.

William just went to the bathroom.

The sun was setting. They ate sandwiches and corn on the cob and strawberries and watermelon.

"When are the fireworks going to start?" asked Olivia.
"When it gets dark," explained her mother.
"When will it be dark?"
"Soon, sweetheart."
"Is it dark yet?"
"Almost. Be patient."

"*Now* is it dark?"

Finally
the fireworks started.

And they were beautiful.

It was very late when everyone got home.

"Go climb into bed, sweetheart," said Olivia's mother.
"No books tonight."

"Aren't you going
to come kiss me
goodnight?"
asked Olivia.

"In a minute — and don't forget to put your band away."

After Ian and William were tucked into bed, Olivia's mother tiptoed into Olivia's room . . .

KINNNK
OOONK
PING
TONG
TING
TANG
CRASH
THUD
KLANG
POINNNNGG
THUMP
PRIIINGG
CRUNCH
BOOOMP

"OLIVIA, I told you to put your band away.
I could have broken my neck!"

But Olivia was fast asleep.

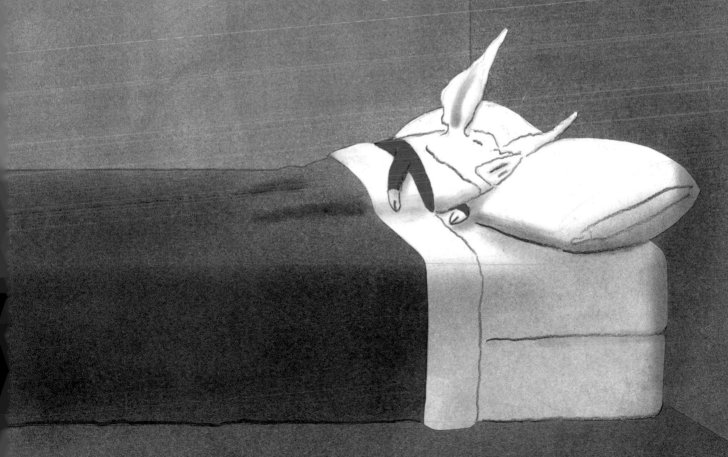

The End